THE PENGUIN CLASSICS

FOUNDER EDITOR: (1944–64) E. V. RIEU

EDITORS:

Robert Baldick (1964–72),
C. A. Jones (1972–4), *Betty Radice*

Abbas Ibn al-Ahnaf was born in 750. His work consists entirely of love poems, a medium which he extended with considerable skill and intelligence. For most of his life he was attached to the court of the Caliph.

Abdullah Ibn al-Mu'tazz, born in 861, was a member of the Abbasid dynasty. Although heir to the Caliphate, he avoided becoming involved in court politics, and devoted his life to poetry and the study of literature He died in 908.

Abu al-Ala al-Ma'arri was born in Ma'rrah, a Syrian country town, in 973. In his twenties his reputation as a poet began to grow, and in 1008 he decided to visit Baghdad which was the cultural capital of the Muslim world. When he left Baghdad his reputation as a poet was established. He returned home, where he attempted to lead the life of an anchorite. He died in 1057.

Abdullah al-Udhari was born in Yemen in 1941 and has lived in England since 1962. He has published translations of poems and short stories in many periodicals. He is a lecturer in Arabic at the Polytechnic of Central London and editor and publisher of *TR*, a bi-lingual Arabic/English literary magazine.

G. B. H. Wightman is a poet who has broadcast for the B.B.C. and produced poetry concerts in England and America. His poems have also been published in numerous English and American journals. He has been Chairman of the Poet's Workshop (1967–9) and is a General Council member of the Poetry Society.

BIRDS THROUGH A
CEILING OF ALABASTER

THREE ABBASID POETS

Arab poetry of the Abbasid Period
translated with an Introduction by
G. B. H. Wightman and
A. Y. al-Udhari

PENGUIN BOOKS

Penguin Books Ltd, Harmondsworth, Middlesex, England
Penguin Books Inc., 7110 Ambassador Road, Baltimore, Maryland 21207, U.S.A.
Penguin Books Australia Ltd, Ringwood, Victoria, Australia
Penguin Books Canada Ltd, 41 Steelcase Road West, Markham, Ontario, Canada
Penguin Books (N.Z.) Ltd, 182–190 Wairau Road, Auckland 10, New Zealand

—

This translation first published 1975
Copyright © G. B. H. Wightman and A. Y. al-Udhari, 1975

—

Made and printed in Great Britain by
Cox & Wyman Ltd,
London, Reading and Fakenham
Set in Monotype Bembo

CONTENTS

The Islamic Empire
from Spain to the borders of China
with principal sites mentioned in the text

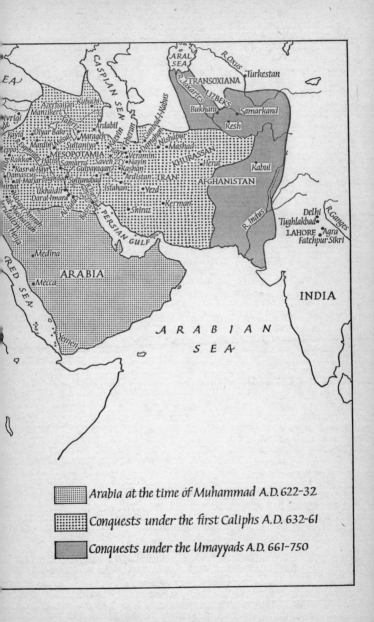

Arabia at the time of Muhammad A.D. 622-32

Conquests under the first Caliphs A.D. 632-61

Conquests under the Umayyads A.D. 661-750

One of the ancient kings of the Yemen built a twenty-storied palace in the northern part of the country. The final ceiling was made of alabaster so that the king could lie and watch the birds flying overhead.

INTRODUCTION

One of the effects of the Prophet Muhammad's teaching was to convert people separated by allegiances to their tribes and chosen idols into an organized force united by the monotheistic Muslim faith. In this climate between 656 and 750 the Umayyad family, formerly opponents of the Prophet, established a centralized government and extended the Arab Empire as far as the Pyrenees in the west and the borders of India and China in the east. The Umayyad's imposition of hereditary rule gave their government, and the Empire itself, an appearance of stability. But in fact the court was no more peaceful than the Tudor court. After enlisting the support of various dissidents, notably in the provinces, the Abbasid family, who were relations of the Prophet, seized power in 750. The Abbasid Period from 750 to 1258 became the Golden Age of Arab Literature.

MAIN PERIODS

The main periods of Arab poetry are usually divided into three stages, namely:

1 Pre-Islamic (Jahiliya)	450–622*
2 Post-Islamic and Umayyad	622–750
3 Abbasid	750–1258

* There are obvious difficulties in dating the origin of poetry in any culture. The ninth-century scholar al-Jahiz (d.869) in his *Kitab al-Hayawan* (*Book of The Animals*) writes: 'As for (Arab) poetry, it is recent. The first to write in this manner, and to pave the way, were Imru al-Qais Ibn Hujr and Muhalhil Ibn Rabi'a. If we examine this poetry, it was 150 years old by the time of the coming of Islam, and at the most 200 years old.'

Dates can never be wholly accurate. It is not only that one school merges into another over a period of time, but also that the earliest written texts of the poets are one to three centuries later than the work they contain. Scholars ascertain when the poems were written by internal evidence – references to a well-known battle, a style of speech, a poetic form – and by the statements of early local historians. Such clues help to fix the dates of poems either exactly or within a time bracket. The scholar's precision is limited by the fact that most of the early poems were handed down by reciters (*rāwīs*) who were both apprentices and the publishers of well-known poets. They are suspected not only of forgetting passages but also of trying to improve them.

PRE-ISLAMIC POETRY

The pre-Islamic poet had a special place in his society. His role was similar to that of the Welsh bard: he praised his prince and acted as the recorder of the tribe's history.

> If you don't believe me ask
>   Anyone who knows our tribe.
> Do they not give all they have
>   To people driven mad by famine
> And drought? We fight with tall spears:
>   They guard the land we protect,
> Their shafts house the weak. In mail
>   Our men are heroes and lords.
>
>   Rabi'a Ibn Maqrum (*c.* 600)

> Ceredig, the loved leader,
> and passionate champion in war,
> the gold-patterned shield of battle:
> spears were splintered and broken,
> like a grown man he held his place with the spears;
> before being pressed down by the earth, before agony,

with his weapons he held his place in the rank.
May he be welcomed in heaven's company
by the Trinity in perfect union.

The men who attacked had lived together,
in their brief lives were drunk on distilled mead;
Mynyddawg's army, famed in battle,
their lives paid for their feast of mead.
Caradawg and Madawg, Pyll and Lewan,
Gwgawn and Gwiawn, Gwyn and Cynvan,
Peredur of steel weapons, Gwawrddar and Aeddan,
attackers in battle, they had their shields broken;
and though they were killed, they killed.
Not one came back to his belongings.
            The Gododdin (c. 580–600) trans. Gwyn Williams*

Early poets, both Arab and Welsh, were believed to possess
magical powers. They were regarded as shamans who could
influence the gods. As a result their advice was frequently
sought on tribal matters. Arab poets also had another function –
to satirize. A poet's skill and invective were employed as a pre-
liminary to battle, the purpose being to shame and to demoralize
the opposing tribe and to enhance and to inspire his own.

Ibn Rashiq, the great eleventh-century scholar and critic,
described the respect accorded the pre-Islamic poet in his *Kitab
al-Umda*:

When a poet was discovered, the other local tribes would come and
visit his family and congratulate them on their good luck ... a poet
was a defence of their honour, a weapon to protect their good name
from insult, a way of making their deeds immortal and a means of
ensuring their fame. They congratulated each other only on three
things – the birth of a son, the emergence of a poet and the foaling of
a fine mare.

In terms of content it is not only praise, exploits and lamenta-
tions which the Arab and Welsh traditions share; there is also a

* Gwyn Williams, *The Burning Tree*, Faber (1956), p. 27.

sharpness of observation which is common to early poetry in most cultures. Where people depend on sight, hearing and grip for survival it is natural that their faculties are likely to be more alert than poets whose days are spent in writing advertising copy or teaching in universities. The pre-Islamic and Welsh poets, while responding to the freshness and individuality of birds, beasts and flowers, invariably introduced them to express a feeling and to make a point. Moreover, they did so within developed verse forms and tight rhyme structures.

The best known verse form of the pre-Islamic period is the *qasida* – a polythematic poem which allows the poet to express a wide range of feelings. The poet begins by addressing the remains of a camp site which he associates with a past love affair.* This part of the *qasida* is called the *nasib*. The poet moves on to praise his horse and to describe his wanderings in the desert. The account of the symbiosis between man and horse is affectionate and particular. The passage as a whole, like Gawain's journey through the Cheshire countryside to meet the Green Knight, evokes the sights and sounds of familiar landscape. The poet next introduces the main subject of the poem which might recount the courage of his patron, the actions of his tribe or his own bravery. He might also add a moral note. The *qasida* thus incorporates in one structure the usual themes of individual early Arab poetry.

---

* 'There is no part of the earth's surface where love exists under such strenuous and endearing conditions as the Arabian desert, where the souls of men and women are knit so closely by the immense isolation of their lives, where either becomes so dependent on the other by the constant pressure of material dangers. Each little "beyt shaar", "house of hair", is as a fortress in the wilderness, set up alone in some far valley against the forces of nature and held there by its dual garrison. In the open plain with its wild, parsimonious beauty, every bush and stone, every beetle and lizard, every rare track of jerboa, gazelle or ostrich on the sand, becomes of value and is remembered, it may be years afterwards, while the stones of the camp-fire stand black and deserted in testimony of the brief season of love.' Wilfred Scawen Blunt, *The Seven Golden Odes of Pagan Arabia*, Chiswick Press (1903), p. xiv.

A poet's ability in the *qasida* form was tested in poetry tournaments held in Mecca and elsewhere during trade fairs. The best, known as the *Mu'allaqat*, are said to have been inscribed in gold and hung in the town's main building. This legend, however, is unlikely because in pre-Islamic times the Ka'ba was a small, roofless enclosure constructed of drystone walls. It was demolished and rebuilt in 608. It is a cube-shaped building and still stands, respected as the holiest place in the Muslim world.

The most famous poets of the pre-Islamic period were Imru al-Qais, Tarafa, Zuhair Ibn Abi Sulma, Labid, Antara, Amr Ibn Kalthum, al-Harith Ibn Hilliza, al-A'sha, Nabigha al-Dhubyani and Abid Ibn al-Abras. Each is said to have had one of his *qasida* or odes on display in the Ka'ba. Shanfara, who was a bandit and not represented in the Ka'ba, is another worthwhile poet of the period. Shanfara's reputation was established by his short poems, his *qit'as* which dealt with famine and poverty, as much as by his *qasidas*.

As poetry was subject to public examination the traditional *qasida* tended, with notable exceptions, to become standardized and to lose the vigour, variety and freshness of its main exponents. The imagery of Imru al-Qais, who is the Chaucer of Arab literature, was especially copied. Imru al-Qais is regarded as the poet who fully developed the *qasida* form and who introduced the opening *nasib* section.*

POST-ISLAMIC AND UMAYYAD POETRY

Muhammad died in 632. He was succeeded by his father-in-law Abu Bakr (d. 634) who was the first Caliph or, literally, Deputy of the Prophet. Initially Caliphs were appointed by a process of consultation. The second Caliph, Umar (d. 644), was murdered

* In the *Diwan* of Imru al-Qais, however, Imru al-Qais is quoted as saying that an earlier poet, Ibn Khidham, employed this device.

by a slave. He was followed by Uthman (d. 656), a member of the Umayyad family. His nephew Mu'awiya (d. 680) had been appointed Governor of Syria by Umar. Mu'awiya ruled over a stable province with a sound central authority and a trained army. When Ali (d. 661), the fourth Caliph, sought to dismiss him, Mu'awiya challenged his authority to do so. After Ali's murder by the Kharjites, a group of religious militants, Mu'awiya took complete control of the Empire. He imposed a form of hereditary rule and the Umayyad dynasty governed for just under a hundred years.

It might be expected that post-Islamic poetry would reflect the impact of Muhammad's teaching. This is only partially true. Some religious poetry did result, but the main body of work remained secular, and emphatically so. It is possible that the conflict which inevitably arose between Islam and the poet's desires acted as a spur. Poetry became both an outlet and a cry of defiance, the cry being an admission of that humanity which Islam wished to discipline. Thus whereas in pre-Islamic times wine poetry was simply celebratory, in post-Islamic times it became invested with an element of tension. On the other hand Islam gave poets, and the Arab language, new concepts, new perspectives and new responses. The concept of love, for example, was expanded and gained a spiritual dimension. War and death likewise took on larger meanings. To die for one's faith, for instance, guaranteed entry to heaven.

Arab conquest and trade also had a substantial if invisible influence. For a number of reasons – partly for religious purposes, partly to consolidate the unity achieved by Muhammad, partly to keep certain warlike tribes occupied, partly to suborn others who threatened rebellion, partly to gain more living space and partly to build up their revenue – the Caliphs who succeeded the Prophet first defeated those Arab tribes which were not toeing the line, and then swept through Iraq, Syria and Egypt. It was a good time to attack. The Byzantine and the Sasanid (Persian) empires, weakened by mutual conflict and lacerated by defensive wars, were easy prey. 'Thus at the very moment when a new invader mobilized in the South', wrote J. F. C. Fuller, 'the two great empires in the East lay exhausted; their territories ravaged, their manpower wasted, their wealth gone; they were a vacuum ready to be filled by the followers of the Prophet.'* With conquest came trade, and with trade came wealth and the growth of towns. Like England in 1560, it was a period of excitement and expansion. The parallel, however, is not exact. The change from a brutal nomadic existence lived in tents, and survival on what was hunted and grubbed, to a town life with houses, mosques and libraries, furniture and ornaments, writing, music and painting, wine and set meals was a much greater change than that experienced by the Elizabethans. The move from polytheism to theism also has no equivalent.

With the growth of towns (Damascus, Medina, Mecca, Kufa and Basra) poets began to write as well as recite their work. Poetry acquired an urban polish and with it an alteration in tone. There were other slow-working changes. The traditional *qasida* ceased to be relevant and was adapted to suit a new environment. Poets wrote more individual and occasional poems. Under the Umayyads love poetry and wine poetry developed. The period sees the rise of the *naqa'id*, a form of

* Major-General J. F. C. Fuller, *The Decisive Battles of the Western World*, Eyre and Spottiswoode (Publishers) Ltd (1954). The Arabs eventually conquered Spain and advanced as far as Aquitaine, until they were defeated at the Battle of Tours in 732. Gibbon wrote of the consequences of this battle: 'A victorious line of march had been prolonged above a thousand miles from the rock of Gibraltar to the banks of the Loire; the repetition of an equal space would have carried the Saracens to the confines of Poland and the Highlands of Scotland: The Rhine is not more impassible than the Nile or Euphrates, and the Arabian fleet might have sailed without a naval combat into the mouth of the Thames. Perhaps the interpretation of the Koran would now be taught in the schools of Oxford, and her pupils might demonstrate to a circumcised people the sanctity and truth of the revelation of Mahomet.' *The Decline and Fall of the Roman Empire*, vol. 6.

satire in which a poet, like Pope or Dryden, attacks his rivals. It also witnesses the emergence of polemical verse. Poets represented the aspirations of religious and political parties. Each one of these genres has antecedents in pre-Islamic times.

There were two sets of Umayyad love poets, both influenced like Thomas Wyatt by music and a wish to set their poems to music. Both schools are known for the narrative characteristics of their lyrics. Poets such as Umar Ibn Abi Rabi'a, al-Ahwas, al-Arji, Ibn Qais al-Ruqayyat and Waddah al-Yaman were famous for their love lyrics, or *ghazal*, which were written in a simple and conversational manner. These poets are associated with the Meccan school of lyric which is engaged and erotic. One of the unusual features of the Meccan school is that they wrote love poems spoken by a mistress and addressed to the poet. The best known representative of this indulgence was Umar Ibn Abi Rabi'a. The Udhri or Bedouin school practised a more self-pitying, platonic lyric in which the poet is a martyr to an unattainable mistress who idealizes all his hopes. Whereas the Meccan school relates more to positive action these lyrics establish a charged mood. The tone and language are more country than town and the poetry is distinguished by a natural simplicity. The work of Jamil Buthaina, Kuthaiyyir Azza, Majnun Laila and Qais Lubna exemplifies this genre. The names Buthaina, Azza, Laila and Lubna are the names of the women the poets loved.

Perhaps the best known poets of the Umayyad period, however, are al-Akhtal, al-Farazdaq and Jarir. The latter two were deadly rivals and their *naqa'ids*, their satirical invectives, which they flung at each other, were recited everywhere; each poet, like a sports hero today, had his host of partisan supporters. Akhtal, an unruly Christian, sided with Farazdaq and also exchanged insults with Jarir. All three poets wrote other kinds of poetry, especially panegyrics and propaganda for their patrons. Akhtal is also known for his wine poetry.

In 750 the Abbasid family, who were descendants of an uncle of the Prophet, challenged and defeated the Umayyads in the Battle of the Great Zab. They came to power with the help of dissidents from the East, reinforced by religious propaganda and economic unrest. The Abbasids strengthened their control by executing the most dangerous of their followers, hunting down survivors of the Umayyad dynasty,* investing their rule with spiritual and ceremonial authority and establishing a sound economic base and administration. They built Baghdad, their capital, on the confluence of the Euphrates and the Tigris. Ships from all parts of the civilized world – from Russia, China, India, Malaya, Africa, Turkey and Syria – anchored at the wharves. The wealth that came to Bhagdad was the source of legend which exists to this day. There was, however, another side of the coin. Many of the subject nations felt themselves exploited. Poets not in court favour wrote of their poverty and the struggle to survive. The exploited and the poor always had political vehicles for their discontent. Just as disputes arose and continued as to the true descendants of the Prophet, the arbitrary Abbasid manner of succession created an ever-increasing number of claimants to the Caliphate. An Abbasid Caliph might appoint his brother, his third son or his cousin as his successor simply on grounds of preference. The disappointed claimants could then be used to front the protests and the demands of the mutinous subjects. Therefore, although the Abbasid period is one of the most brilliant and astonishing civilizations, one marked by lasting achievements in the arts, sciences and learning, and one which continues to permeate, it was never calm.

The Umayyad poets had shown their new status as individual

* Some of the Umayyads, and in particular Abdul Rahman, escaped and re-established the Umayyad rule in Spain.

citizens, in contrast to their former status as common members of a tribe, by escaping from the embracing hold of the *qasida* and moving towards writing particular poems on subjects which personally interested them. It was a period of development. The Abbasid poets built upon this work.

Bashshar Ibn Burd (d. 783), Salih Ibn Abd al-Quddus (d. 783), Abu al-Shamaqmaq (d. 796) and Ibn Harma (d. 792) are regarded as the first exemplars of the Abbasid poetic tradition. The former two poets were both blind, both condemned as heretics and both executed by the Caliph al-Mahdi in the same year. While Ibn Burd wrote largely in the *qasida* mode, both introduced a critical and questioning note into their poetry which was directed at religious orthodoxy, but simultaneously helped to undermine literary convention. Abu al-Shamaqmaq's obscene verse, his declarations of poverty and his broadsides against injustice had a similar subversive effect. Most of these poets, especially Ibn Burd and Ibn Harma, consciously exploited poetic technical devices, known as *badi*, such as metaphor, alliteration, personification, hyperbole, assonance, dissonance, puns and wit. Other poets, like Hammad Ajred (d. 778) and Muti' Ibn Iyas (d. 786), advocated sybaritic indulgence and used everyday language which mimed their philosophy. They too played a part in directing future poets to new possibilities.

A host of factors contributed to the richness of Abbasid verse. The Middle East was the womb of many civilizations, of which the most recent were the Sasanid (Persian), the Byzantine, the Jewish, the Aramaic and the Christian. Conquest and trade brought a further infusion of thought and styles from Greece, Italy, India and China. In the face of this competition, and borrowing from it, Arab scholars established universities to develop their own religion, sciences and literature. Philological schools promoted a tradition of Arab poetry by collecting, collating and setting down past oral epics and fragments. They were also responsible for hammering out syntactical rules for written Arabic and guidelines for the civil service or secretarial class. A policy of patronage – the acceptable face of despotism – was pursued not only by the Caliph of Baghdad, but also by provincial governors and rich merchants.

Briefly, the wealth, the diversity of races, the amalgam of cultures and the new ideas which flooded into Baghdad during this period led to an assault on established values, the encouragement of hedonism and innovation in art. Abu Nuwas (d. 810) is possibly the paradigm of the age. A complex and obsessed character, he openly mocked the *qasida*, gloried in hunting, wine, and boys, successfully experimented with many forms and wrote vividly. It is an identifying characteristic of the 'new poets' that their poetry – in defiance of those scholars who held that pre-Islamic verse was the only well of virtue – used natural speech. So much was this the case that certain expressions which were colloquial then remain colloquial today. A contemporary, Abu al-Atahiya (d. 828), known for his grave and hypocritical poetry, said: 'The diction of a poet should not be the kind which people have to stop and think about. This is especially true of moral poetry such as mine. Morality is not kingly, nor does it belong to reciters of poetry, nor is it the possession of the eclectic. It is a creed which most appeals to ordinary people . . . They best like things they can understand.'

Muslim Ibn al-Walid (d. 824) perfected the musical qualities of the *badi*. This interest in the techniques of poetry, the rhetorical mechanics, was complemented by the development and fruition of numerous stylistic forms. The *qit'a* or short descriptive poem, which had its origin in pre-Islamic times and which was used by the Umayyad poets, gained increasing currency and distinction. Most of the poems in this selection belong to the *qit'a* tradition. Abbas Ibn al-Ahnaf (d. 809), for instance, wrote mostly *qit'as* which he refined.

While other poets may boast, praise and lament on a score of themes, Ahnaf is unique in that his lyrics are exclusively concerned with love. No other poet in the Abbasid period so telescopes his choice of subject matter.

Abbasid poetry, like the Metaphysical poetry after the Elizabethans, ultimately becomes more complex. Concepts are as important as images; ideas as dynamic as events. Abu Tammam (d. 846) was the innovator of this mode. The process was furthered by the growing interest in science seeded by new advances in mathematics, astronomy and philosophy. The study of language by the philological schools inevitably tended to an examination of poetic form and poetic devices. Poetry as an art grew more craft-conscious and thereby more self-conscious. It is indicative that both Abu Tammam and his disciple al-Buhturi (d. 897) produced critical anthologies. Al-Buhturi combined traditional content with new techniques and by his unobtrusive craftsmanship and musical sensitivity matched descriptive beauty with formal beauty. Mutanabbi (d. 965) is regarded as one of the greatest Arab poets. During his lifetime the Caliphate fell into decay and came under foreign rule. Mutanabbi's poetry is protean. He expresses the *Zeitgeist* – the anguish of the homeless individual personifying the lost empire – in textured language powered by a unity of intellect and emotion. He had a gift for integrating his grasp of ideas in such a way that they serve the poem rather than the poem serving them. The work of Abu al-Ala al-Ma'arri (d. 1057), with its philosophical overtones and its moral energy, is the high-water mark both of this period of intellectual dynamism and of the Golden Age as a whole.

It is a feature of mature literatures that the past is liable to be a ballchain on any forward impetus. Traditional forms become outworn and natural images deteriorate into clichés. The language is haunted by echoes and rendered bland by institutional standards and prolonged overwork. In such a situation the poet constantly seeks new vehicles in which to express himself and a fresh diction to make things new. A note of desperation enters into poetry. At this point modish stylistic postures are hailed as new aesthetic developments, extremist content replaces imaginative vision and novelty is pursued for its own sake. There comes a time, often associated with a breakdown in moral structures, when value structures cease to exist. One poem because it is classed as a poem is said to be as good as any other poem. Abbasid poetry did not fall to the level of such banality but after Ma'arri (d. 1057), apart from an excursion into mystical verse, it was arrested by the dead-weight of tradition and stultified by attempts at new forms which lacked the necessary accompanying vision and body. For political and economic reasons patronage lessened and poetry was affected by the orthodoxy of scholars. This decline is matched by a weakening of the central government, a breakdown in trade links, invasion by Bedouins, Turks and Crusaders, and the ultimate destruction in 1258 of the Abbasid Caliphate by the Mongol Prince Hulegu.

Abbas Ibn al-Ahnaf

Abbas Ibn al-Ahnaf was born in 750. He is said to have been a handsome, generous and good-natured man from a well-known family. A nephew, Ibrahim Ibn al-Abbas, describes him as a brilliant conversationalist: 'When he spoke we never wanted him to stop.' There is a story that Harun al-Rashid's Vizier called on Ahnaf to reconcile the Caliph and the Caliph's favourite concubine. The two were angry with each other and pride made it impossible for them to meet. There was an impasse. Ahnaf wrote a short set of verses which brought them together. The concubine agreed to renew the relationship on the condition that Ahnaf was paid. He was prodigally rewarded by the Caliph, by the concubine and by the Vizier, and remained attached to the court. The concubine,

Marida, became the great-grandmother of Ibn al-Mu'tazz.

Ahnaf's work consists entirely of love poems, a medium which he extended with considerable skill and intelligence. They are examples, like the other poems in this selection, of *qit'a*. The latter means literally 'fragments' and refers to short verses which tend, like epigrams, to concentrate upon a single subject or a single theme. Ahnaf's poetry had a formative influence on later poets. Ibn al-Mu'tazz, who was a notable critic as well as a fine poet, stated that Ahnaf's poetry was the best he had read. Another poet, Abu al-Atahiya, wrote: 'I have envied no one except Ahnaf.' It is surprising that as Ahnaf was held in such high esteem both by his contemporaries and by his successors he has received little attention in the West. There is no collection of his work in English.

Ahnaf's poetry is the expression of a mature, humorous sensibility and reflects a wide variety of moods. His irony, hyperbole and concealed desperation are reminiscent of Wyatt and Lovelace, who were also courtiers. Like Wyatt, Ahnaf wrote many of his poems to be set to music. His diction is plain, simple and lively. Yet this simplicity is deceptive. His imagery is so natural we are likely to overlook its originality. When Ahnaf writes

> When she walks with her girl servants
> Her beauty is a moon between swaying lanterns, (p. 41)

the picture he presents is clear, penetrating and immediate. It is also unusual.

In other poems he organizes his metaphors and thought into a highly complex whole, but his artistry is such that we are only conscious of an intrinsic aptness. He constructs these poems like a mobile sculpture: the imagery of one line, or *bait*, is not logically connected with the imagery of another, but placed together the sequence of unexpected relationships establishes an organic sum which in turn creates an overall mood. Something of this technique is seen in the following poem.

> Love has trees in my heart, and they
>   Are watered by pent-up rivers.
>
> The black-eyed girl who's so demure,
>   And speaks coyly like a high flute,
> Nudged sleep from my head. My liver
>   Turned to fire and I cried with pain.
>
> I loved those tears which swamped my eyes,
>   Twin pupils drowned beneath a liquid sky. (p. 38)

Here Ahnaf rapidly switches attention from love, trees, his voice, watering, pent-up rivers, a black-eyed girl, her voice, his lack of sleep, his pain, his tears, his eyes and drowning, until eventually we end with tears resembling a rainy sky which in turn resembles a lake. In other poems he moves from one subject of address to another, and from direct speech to indirect speech, without warning. This technical ploy, these sudden alterations in subject and in empathy, encapsulate in the poem the rapid activity of an intelligent mind under pressure from a variety of emotions. The underlying humour distances the experience and places it in perspective.

Abdullah Ibn al-Mu'tazz

Abdullah Ibn al-Mu'tazz, the second of the three poets, was a member of the Abbasid dynasty. He was born in Samarra in 861, the great-great-grandson of Harun al-Rashid. When he was six weeks old his grandfather, the Caliph al-Mutawakkil, was brutally murdered by the palace guards. Eight years later his father was also murdered. Ibn al-Mu'tazz escaped to Mecca with his grandmother; but after a while he was allowed to return to Baghdad where he grew up. Although heir to the Caliphate, he avoided becoming involved in court politics. He

23

sought to devote his life to poetry and the study of literature. His wealth, being dependent on the whims and tactics of the ruling members of his family, was intermittent. Even so he was usually comfortable and able to lead a frivolous life. After a cousin was deposed, Mu'tazz – in an attempt to end the intrigue, murder and revolution which plagued the court – agreed to assume the throne. He ruled for a day and a night. He then went into hiding, was discovered and strangled. He died in 908.

Mu'tazz is one of the most notable poets of the Abbasid period. Yet little of his poetry exists in translation. Among Western students of Arab literature he is better known as the author of *Kitab al-Badi* – one of the first Arab studies of poetic form. On the other hand Ibn Rashiq (d. 1070) in his classic work, *Treatise on the Art of Poetry*, wrote: 'I do not know a poet who is more perfect and amazing in his craft than Ibn al-Mu'tazz. His art is so light and so delicate it can scarcely be detected.'

Although Mu'tazz's art may be imperceptible, his quality is apparent. Frequently he concentrates upon an intense visual experience in a surprising metaphor or simile. We derive pleasure not only from the economy and brilliance of expression, but also from the fact that he makes us see physical objects from a different angle. They are made new and, an interesting epistemological point, the result is more accurate than most descriptions. There are few English poets who see the world quite so sharply. It is arguable that the clarity of light in the Middle East, in contrast to the subtleties of shade in northern Europe, is responsible for this distinction.

Mu'tazz, reflecting his princely background, is a hedonist. In one or two longer poems he deplores the unrest which afflicts his country. In the *qit'as* we have translated, apart from visual enjoyment, he delights in friendship, drink and women. His delight is civilized by a worldly irony and elevated by a keen sense of beauty. His perfected art is the outward sign, and exemplum, of this aesthetic instinct. His intelligence and discipline save his poetry from triviality and flabbiness to which many poets who share his outlook are prone. In this respect he has much in common with Herrick.

Abu al-Ala al-Ma'arri

Abu al-Ala al-Ma'arri was born in Ma'rrah, a Syrian country town, in 973. His life is well documented and a collection of his letters survives. When he was four years old he suffered an attack of smallpox and became blind. His father died when he was fourteen. At about this time Ma'arri began six years' intensive study. He visited Aleppo, Antioch and other Syrian towns, several of which had libraries with up to 20,000 volumes. Ma'arri learnt many of these by heart and attended lectures by famous scholars. It is significant that like his father and other members of his family he avoided making the customary pilgrimage to Mecca. When he was twenty he returned home and lived in comparative poverty, during which period his reputation as a poet began to grow.

In 1008, when he was about thirty-five, Ma'arri decided to visit Baghdad, the cultural capital of the Muslim world. Here through public recitation a poet could obtain an international name and a solid living as a writer of laudatory verses. However, Ma'arri had a distaste for patrons and so, despite the fact that his talent was recognized, his stay was financially insecure. After eighteen months he returned home. Ma'arri said that he did not wish to leave and that the reason for his departure was the death of his mother. Some of his contemporaries thought that the real reason was his failure to establish himself in the city, combined with a humiliation inflicted upon him by a local nobleman. The story is that in a disagreement over the work of Mutanabbi, a famous poet of the previous century, the nobleman had Ma'arri dragged out of the room by his ankles.

At home Ma'arri led an ascetic and vegetarian existence: he lived on lentils and figs and remained confined to his house for the rest of his days. Bound by blindness and four walls he was known as the man of two prisons. When Ma'arri added his lack of religion to these two privations he referred to himself as a person who experienced 'three nights'. His attempt to be an anchorite was only partially successful. His house became an object of pilgrimage and disciples from all over the educated world came to visit him and hear him speak. He gave seminars on poetry and rhetoric and, although his verse is marked by misanthropy, earned many friends and took a kindly interest in their writing.

Western scholars and critics have given a lot of attention to Ma'arri's work. R. A. Nicholson, perhaps his best known interpreter, has written: 'His work should be weighed by the standard which we apply to the *Divina Commedia* or the *Paradise Lost*. He sits below Dante and Milton, but he belongs to their school.'* Many would disagree with Nicholson and argue that Ma'arri is their equal. (There is a reputable theory that Dante was indebted to his Arab predecessor.)

Ma'arri's poetry reflects the mind of a man who continues to think about the serious questions of life without coming to a final conclusion. In one poem he asserts that there is no life after death, in another poem he says that we cannot be sure. His probing scepticism, his resolution not to seek shelter in a philosophical formula, is a mark of Ma'arri's greatness and gives his work a lasting relevance. The speculative inconsistency is a pleasingly human quality and modifies the bleakness of his outlook.

Critics have complained that Ma'arri's view of mankind and the world is unduly black; but recollecting his own afflictions and the conditions of the time, in which war, famine, lawlessness

* R. A. Nicholson, *Studies in Islamic Poetry*, Cambridge University Press (1921), p. 44.

and corruption were the order of the day, his pessimism and misanthropy had ample justification. His attitude to humanity, and his concept of its significance within the universe, resembles that of the American poet Robinson Jeffers who advised his children, 'Be in nothing so moderate as in love of man', and who wrote, describing the Pacific:

> ... this is the staring unsleeping
> Eye of the earth; and what it watches is not our wars.*

Unlike Jeffers, Ma'arri goes beyond negative rejection and introduces a positive moral recommendation. Truth and morality are twin obsessions. He wrote: 'I have not sought to embellish my verse by means of fiction or fill my pages with love idylls, battle scenes, descriptions of wine parties and the like. My aim is to speak the truth.' With mock humility he adds: 'Now, the proper end of poetry is not truth but falsehood, and in proportion as it is diverted from its proper end its perfection is impaired. Therefore I must crave indulgence of my readers for this book of *moral* poetry.'†

Armed with this policy, and remarkable gifts of wit, satire and epigram, he lashes – with an occasional weather-eye cocked in the direction of religious and political authorities – at man's pretensions and follies. Ma'arri's polemic is noteworthy. Milton, when he chastises wickedness, sustains a lofty tone. Ma'arri in contrast rolls up his sleeves and attacks his targets brutally.

In many areas Ma'arri was much in advance of his time and a courageous outsider. He scorned religion, not simply the Muslim faith, but all religious institutions. He likewise despised those who depended upon religion, believing that they should

---

* From 'The Eye' in *Robinson Jeffers: Selected Poems*, Random House Inc., N.Y. (1963).

† R. A. Nicholson, *Studies in Islamic Poetry*, Cambridge University Press (1921), p. 50.

rely, as he did, upon reason and their own inner resources. Yet
sometimes he is dubious of his own scepticism:

> I advise you to avoid ugliness
> And do what's good; for I've learnt the soul
> Near death repents, repents its gouty skin
> Which began so fresh, and may do again. (p. 102)

ON TRANSLATION

There has recently been a boom in translation. Whether this is
because English poets have become more outward-looking or
the world smaller, it is difficult to say. It is more likely to be yet
another instance of the long tradition of translation, and
imitation, which has existed since Chaucer. Indeed on reflection
it is hard to find a serious poet who has not engaged in trans-
lation. In the recent past Pound, Eliot, Jones, Auden, Lowell
and Heath-Stubbs have ransacked foreign literatures.

An interest in translation always gives rise to an interest in
the nature of translation. The ancient questions of what a
translated poem keeps and what it loses in the passage from one
language to another, from one age to another, from one
milieu to another, and from one mind to another are questions
about psychology as much as they are questions about linguis-
tics, and cannot be adequately answered within the space of a
short introduction.

On the other hand, it may be useful to set down what we
have sought to keep and what we have agreed to lose in
translation. We have sought to communicate the spirit, tone,
diction and content of the Arab originals. In short, we have
tried to capture the individual voice of each of our poets. There
is a gap of 300 years between Ahnaf and Ma'arri. If we look at
English literature over a similar period, we have poets as
various as Herrick, Milton, Pope, Wordsworth and Dylan

Thomas. It is therefore unlikely that while Ahnaf, Mu'tazz and Ma'arri are Arabs, they will replicate one another. This point unfortunately needs to be made because many of us approach Arab literature with a preconceived notion of its character. Poets such as James Elroy Flecker have conditioned us to expect a richly larded style when in fact the original is quite likely to be distinguished by a cleanliness of line and a conversational tone.

We have agreed to sacrifice form, rhyme, metre and sound. The reason we have done so is because the Arab language is categorically separate from the English language. It is not an Aryan tongue; it is Semitic. Moreover the poetic tradition – the map of connotations, imagery and verbal conventions – is different.

In the case of form, a typical poem is written as follows:

نقومي فان انست كذبتنسي   بقولي فاسئل بقومي عليمـا

اليسوالذين اذا ازمــة   الحت على الناس تنسي الحلوما

يهينون في الحق اموالعـم   اذا اللزبات التحين المسهما

طوال الرماح غداة الصباح   ذوو نجدة يمنعون الجريها

بنوالحرب يوماذا استلا‌موا   حسبتهم في الحد يد القروسا

The Arab language goes from right to left. Whereas this may be of interest to a concrete poet, it is not a feature which can otherwise be sensibly adapted into English. An Arab verse line is usually divided into two complementary halves. The first is called *sadar*, the breast; and the second is called *ajz*, the buttock. The two halves, or distich, invariably contain a rhyme-pattern with an emphasis on the monorhyme which comes at the end of the second half throughout the poem. This is the traditional *qasida* pattern which goes as follows:

```
a——————    a——————
a——————    b——————
a——————    c——————
a——————    d——————
```

Given the limited rhyme potential in English in contrast to the abundant potential in Arabic, and the dangers of obviousness and predictability in English rhyme, one cannot imitate the pattern of the original without damaging the effect and truth of the total poem.

The metre in Arab verse is quantitative with long and short syllables. There are sixteen metres in traditional Arab poetry, and each metre has a set of variations. However, it is impossible to communicate these metres and metrical variations successfully because the sound of the language has no equivalence in English. The first letter of a common word such as *hub*, meaning 'love', cannot be pronounced in English. In the word *qatr*, which is the Arabic for 'dew' or 'raindrops', the phonic qualities of the *q* and the *t* are wholly foreign to the English throat and the English ear.

In seeking to capture the individual voice of the poets, the English we have chosen to employ can, *via negativa*, firstly be described in the styles we have tried to avoid. There are four types of vehicle commonly found in translations, namely, university English, Georgian English, pastiche English and translation English.

University English is leaden, dictionary accurate and poetically wrong. Randall Jarrell once remarked that nobody thinks that some professor of Lithuanian could have written *Anna Karenina*, but everyone thinks he is the ideal man to translate it. He is too harsh. Certain academics, the late Professor A. J. Arberry for example, make up in enthusiasm and devotion what they lack in pulse and skill. They are cartographers who show us the way rather than explorers who report what the landscape is like.

Georgian English, to give a stipulative definition, is *kitsch* English. Just as Landseer's cats, dogs and monkeys continue to adorn birthday cards, so the legacy of the worst Georgian verse (which must never be confused with the excellent best) persists in certain translations, although possibly to a lesser extent now. It is a type of slack writing in which the translator by the use of inversions, romantic imagery and rhyme, signals that his work is meant to be poetry. The potency of Landseer's animals and Georgian diction is hard to understand; but nevertheless anyone who has judged a poetry competition will confirm the strength of the latter's lasting hold.

Pastiche English is appliqué English. It is used in translations to make the verse seem modern. Such translations are usually sprinkled with four-letter words, contain references to television and are strenuously contrived. Some translations, Porter's 'After Martial' for instance, possess the wit, aptness and skill to render the original in terms of the contemporary without strain. But such performances are rare.

Translation English is model English and hard to fault. It is smooth, ordered and consistent. It is the BBC voice of translation. It communicates with level precision. Such English, however, lacks vitality and character. It does not convey the heartbeat of the original poem. Moreover it is too limited an instrument to handle the translator's delicate art of symbiosis whereby he seeks to transmit the natural and often vernacular voice of the ancient poet in the accent of the present. Obviously no such aspirations can be wholly fulfilled. There is a ceiling of alabaster between the darting swifts and the translator.

Therefore in trying to communicate the spirit, tone, diction and content of the Arab originals the language we have chosen is the language of today, with an ear to the recondite nuances which give our speech its hidden code, its subtle inflexions and its temporal identity: nuances which derive from the playground, bus queues and offices as well as from the media, books and our poetic tradition. The translator requires to calibrate his inner ear to match the information he receives through his outer ear. This is not to say that the translator should rely upon, or even have a special bias towards, demotic speech; but on the other hand, unless he notices, understands and appreciates his own verbal environment, he cannot express the thought and temper of the original poet.

There is a clinching factor for choosing vital diction rather than literary diction. A translator has to appreciate the language of his time in order to write a contemporary poem; and he has to write a contemporary poem in order to achieve a worthwhile poetic translation. The successful translation of an eighth-century Arab poem must be a successful twentieth-century poem.

We have stressed the matter of language because it is important to overcome the false belief that Arab literature is luscious. The language of many Abbasid poets is conversational; and where in other instances it is heightened, there is a bedrock of common speech. Naturally, while laying stress on common speech, Wordsworth's language of men, we do not wish to imply that it should be used crudely. Speech, like clay or steel, requires art to create the object desired; or, in the case of translation, to imitate the object already created. Whether or not the translations contained in this selection satisfy the criteria established is another matter.

The translator's role is a humble one. His work is an act of respect. No matter how scrupulous he is, no matter how inspired he may be, he knows that the nature of translation is such that the end result can never be perfect. Moreover he realizes that his own efforts are only secondary. The dead poet is the prime mover. He also usually realizes that he owes his knowledge of the period and his access to the text to the work of others who have preceded him. Where the translation of Arab poetry is concerned, scholars and enthusiasts such as William Jones, Charles Lyall, Wilfred Blunt, H. A. R. Gibb, A. J. Arberry and especially R. A. Nicholson have already beaten a path.

ABBAS IBN AL-AHNAF

(750-809)

When I visit you and the moon
   Isn't around to show me the way,
Comets of longing set my heart
   So much ablaze, the earth is lit
By the holocaust under my ribs.

You've never really suffered, or known
   The anguish of insomnia.
It is I who can never sleep,
   And while I live, I cannot stop
The tears welling out of my eyes.

You scorn me when I speak to you,
   Yet lovers who quote my verse succeed.
I've become a candle thread destined
   To light a room for other men
While burning away into thin air.

She is formed complete
   And beauty is complete
In her face; beauty
   Which lies not in her face
Lacks beauty's total.
   Once a month people see
A new moon in the sky.
   Every dawn I hold
A new moon in her face.

Love has trees in my heart, and they
  Are watered by pent-up rivers.

The black-eyed girl who's so demure,
  And speaks coyly like a high flute,
Nudged sleep from my head. My liver
  Turned to fire and I cried with pain.

I loved those tears which swamped my eyes,
  Twin pupils drowned beneath a liquid sky.

Zalum said, and she was never unfair,
    The man who compared me to the moon
Was mistaken: the moon has no damson eyes,
    Nor idle charm that makes for boredom.

The heart, moved by love, wants to fly.
My chest holds an outburst of wings,
The hands of a tambourine girl.

When she walks with her girl servants,
Her beauty is a moon between swaying lanterns.

She abandoned my beating heart,
And it flounders in the mere of absence.

Tell Narjess she must rescue her victim,
Or be found guilty of murder by neglect.

After she'd sown love in my heart,
She became unobtainable.

The heart is a hectare of love,
An orchard of prickly tragacanth trees.

Seeing you brought trouble, headaches day and night.
There's no sense loving a girl who cuts you.

She's the sun living at home in the sky.
Therefore be consoled; a beautiful thought –

While you can't reach her level, she won't hit yours.

I'm drawn to what's harmful, it infects my system.
When a friend sees me, weak and flushed, he thinks
        'Poor man,
I'll soon mourn his passing.'

The sneak who told her of this illness placed my life
In careless hands. How can I live? My blood carries
The virus I avoid:

Despair knocks down lovers quicker than cholera.

Bear in mind how I stand in your courtyard,
Perplexed, your scent drifting from a window.

When shoes clack, I turn my head left and right,
Like one overboard desperate for a line.

Abbas I wish you were the shirt
  On my body, or I your shirt.

Or I wish we were in a glass
  You as wine, I as rainwater.

Or I wish we were two love birds
  Who lived alone in the desert,

No people.

Not having her I'm angry; anxious too.
I'm tired, tired, no sleep; even now I can't rest.
My worries are snakes, my body their pit.

When an idle man tastes love, he rubs his eyes;
(If she accepts him, his dumb look returns).

The lover pictures the girl he adores
Listening in her room to his cauldron words.

Love is a bell which startles the lazy mind;
As I put up my feet, I hear it clang.

Listen I'll tell you a strange tale.
A friendly woman I know
Sent a note by messenger.
She mocked me for your coldness;
You'll never guess what I wrote.

Souls die when their hour is due,
But mine stops before its time,

Though it hurts, I keep away,
For she'll get bored if I call.

When chasing days make me sad,
   I don't think about myself;
I'll live as long as I should.
   It's because time may change you
I fear sunsets and feel lost.

Let me die. I brought nothing new to love,
Nor am I unique in suffering people's scorn.

When you told me she'd left, your gentle approach
Seemed to say death and parting are the same.

I'm sorry for those who showed me friendship,
My grateful response quickly made them numb.

I rose when they came, their love on my back,
But they sat down without a word or nod.

They wronged me. I've not received the favour
I was led to expect. When I am gone,

No one will feel the way I felt for you;
These days my permanent friend is worry.

All I hope is you'll learn how my heart loved you,
And hear the silent voice of my true self.

The mark of two people in love; they argue
   All the time, right or wrong, on every point.

Watch how their tongues battle, their love reconciles,
   Their desire pains – so intensely, they cry.

The man who reproaches you is unfair;
  You're a woman and not a saint.

His voice, when she hears him, betrays
  A fatal tone. I stoop to love,

And live resigned to the nature
  God's written me. I don't break promises,
My heart is not cold like your heart.

I've experienced all the hardships of life,
But love's far and away the worst I've known.

The misery Harut and his friend suffered
Is almost sweet compared to the torture

Of people who need a friend. Love has a glass
Full of liquid fear; we all sip that drink.

If it'll please you, I'll die of depression;
My mouth, shut at last, won't upset your moods.

Once I felt you turned to me as a friend,
But now you turn aside. Life's altered you.

That natural law of change, decay and death
Works within us all; but you cannot wait

To see me go. I hope God cripples your haste.

Since her impact, my heart shoots up and down
Flying between sand and cloud, cloud and sand.

What's wrong with love? It disturbs the piety
Of God's servants. He shouldn't feather those darts.

Love's saddled me with a reticent woman
Who uses veil and shutter for defence.

Daily I stood by her door, wanting her;
So long I became a nail in the wood.

My dear, is your heart true or false?
   It is false. You promised

To love me but the evidence
   I was shown proves you broke your word.

Don't ask my heart to love you more:
   From its ground a spring burst like blood.

This daughter of Eve, how marvellous she looks;
Life would lack sparkle if you left, comfort too.

Listen, if you saw her, you'd always be young:
No wrinkles scoop your face, no grey tint your hair.

Will I meet her? No, I don't hope that much;
It won't hurt if you talk in your letters.

Give me your hand and let's be friends once more;
And let's jointly curse whoever was wrong.
Please answer my note; your reply will cure
My depression. Oh love, I send salaams –
As many as the stars, and birds flying.

On the road to her house, I was ambushed
By outlaw Night, then struck by suave Darkness.

A lone star in the quarry of the sky
Became a blind man ditched without a guide.

Who destroyed my sleep by closing her eyes
And won't see the agony her rest causes?

You've made my irises uncurtained windows;
Why must they stare? Let my sleep bless your sleep.

I almost wore a doctor's robe
So I could come to you on call

And God would let me near you once.

ABDULLAH IBN AL-MU'TAZZ

(861-908)

Night has fallen about us my friend,
    Light our fire with wine
So, while the world sleeps, we may kiss
    The sun in the dark.

Watch now the beauty of the crescent moon as it
    ascends,
Ripping the darkness with its light; look, a scythe of
    silver
Mowing a black prairie that's clustered with white
    narcissi.

And the lemon on its branch is true gold;
A coloured ball which once struck hangs in flight
For an eye blink, still poised on the swung polo stick.

The narcissus stares without once
    Resting its eyes; its back is bent
By still raindrops, its face is pale
    Watching how the sky chastens the earth.

With streams of wine the garden is crossed,
  And the doves sing higher and higher.
Do not blame the branches if they dance,
  They are drunk with song and liquor.

Thank God, the new moon,
  Ramadan has gone.
Quick, lash out the wine;
  The moon's a silver dhow
Laden with chunks of amber.

The eyelids of the burdened cloud let fall cascades
Of rain, and the parterred garden is spattered with drops.
You see the exact spot when each hits the hoed ground:
It's like silver coins which bounce, are snatched, yet leave
A mark. So often the rain slaps the cheek of the earth.
There are running streams and the garden newly
          blossoms.

The cavalry of dew is mounted on flowers
  Stirred by the whip of the wind.

The field gallops as it stands.

The sun rose above the stream
    Whose calm water quivered when the east wind blew;

Fantasies of golden armour.

When fire is fanned,
Wood and charcoal;

Flames rise like cedars of gold.

You've seen a moonlit night
   Silver the streets of a town;
And wine pure as sun flecks,
   The glass turbanned with foam.

I don't want to drink in ruins under a sky
   The belly of a wild ass.

Nor under a roof that sieves rain with broken walls
   Which let in great mounds of soil.

I want to drink in the morning when heaven appears
   Wearing a kaftan of voile;

And the Eastern breeze goes for a stroll through a garden
   Full of blossom lapped with dew;

And the bright sun is like a newly minted dinar.

Bring a bottle, Saki,* and let's be happy.
  You've seen the night depart and the dawn flash
Like a meteor; the Pleiades, seven glasses,
  Have come and gone. You, Saki, are the East
Decanting wine, and the West drinks your warmth.

* Winebearer.

The yellow Karkhiyah* burns in its beaker;
A dash of water turns to molten glass,

And the goblet hard ice.

When the sky's eyelids had disfigured the earth
  With a rapid downpour of stormy tears,

The sun touched the world and the plains appeared
  In silk brocade, the hills a veil of water.

We must meet only after dark.
  The sun is a gossip, but night
A pimp whose bordello curtains

Shield many trysts.

It's like my heart was in the talons of a hawk
   Which one morning dropped, soared and never
      returned.

When it wants prey, the hawk stirs; its wings start to flap,
   A man in a cloak who runs across a courtyard.

It claws the heart, its talons are hooks laced with twine
   And knotted at the ankle. Agh . . .

Moving fast a girl came to me one night
   Hurrying to abscond from innocence.

When she walked, her body said to the wind,
   If you're serious, this is the way you should stir

The branches.

A wonderful night, but so short
I brought it to life, then strangled it:

A shirt I fold and put aside.

Time, you haven't left me a friend,
  There's no kindness in your life.

You devour my companions,
  Then greet me with insolence.

Let the man who brings you to me be given
   What he wants. Why are you angry?

Guards protect you from my approaches. I dream,

Perfect as a branch, and your face the sun
   That shines all day through your body.

Without being called, her image cured me,
My loss changed to a sense of nearness.

Sleep's an old whore who brings my love to bed
From where she warmly lies, however far.

When my friends passed out that evening
 The sparkle of wine bubbles entranced me,
The soft talk of the reed and lute.
 Night was about to throw meteors
At my blurred head, and scream, 'Quisling!'

It's the pilgrim season
  In the square of Mecca,
And at Yasiriyah
  The lovers congregate.
As a money dealer
  Tests his coin, I read faces.

Her lock-covered face the lost moon.

The chaperon they paid got drunk
And watched me in his dreams; she stayed

Teaching me the taste of her mouth.

Delays in Baghdad worried me;
  Journeys seldom turn out as planned.

I was detained too long in town,
  A eunuch clutched by an old crone.

If you're rich, then you're unlucky;
All you need is a face which says

I'm a descendant of Adam.

You tortured me with postponements
    And weak excuses. You mustn't despise
A man's grey hair. It is your work.

The night I worried stretched so long,
  I felt the sun had joined the stars.

We drowned in waves of rain
   (Someone else prayed for it).
The sun with rheumy eyes
   Tries to break the soft cloud
Like a eunuch struggling
   To enter a virgin.

ABU AL-ALA AL-MA'ARRI

(973-1057)

Some people are like an open grave:
You give it the thing you love most
And then get nothing in return.

A man hard done by, yet generous,
Is a rock on which light rain falls;
Tufts of moss grow, but flowers won't bloom.

Tear down every dwelling on earth.
Each houses creatures who'll destroy
The untamed soul of a good man.

Hold tight to what is most yourself,
Don't squander it, don't let your life
Be governed by what disturbs you.

You're given the fruit of one palm tree:
Bear it a basin of clear water.
Don't trouble with the plight of other palms.

When they struck camp, my people left in my heart
A revolving planet that's slow to fade.

My trial of darkness seems so long I roar:
'When will the black curled night whiten into day?

Tell me, have the wings of that star been clipped?
Its body turns in space, but won't take flight.'

They say the soul's ferried corpse to infant
Till, cleansed by each crossing, it's fit for God.

Don't believe what you're told unless your mind
Confirms its truth: palm trunks, lofty as clouds,

Stay wood. Be calm, take care and bear in mind
The Indian sword is worn thin as it's honed.

The comet, has it nerves or is it dead;
Has it a mind, or is it burning rock?

Some people believe in a world after death,
While others say we're only vegetables.

I advise you to avoid ugliness
And do what's good, for I've learnt the soul

Near death repents, repents its gouty skin
Which began so fresh, and may do again.

We laughed; our laughing betrayed scorn.
People on this earth should live in fear.
When men shake hands with time, time crushes
Them like tumblers; little pieces of glass.

God help us, we have sold our souls, all that was best,
To an enterprise in the hands of the Receiver.
We've no dividends, or rights, for the price we paid.
Yet should our wills choose between this corrupt business
And a paradise to come, rest assured they'd want

The world we have now.

If the intellect is unstable
It is overwhelmed by the world,
A weak man embraced by a whore.

If the mind becomes disciplined,
The world is a distinguished woman
Who rejects her lover's advances.

If your home is a prison,
Then your tomb must be a fort.

If this life degrades your mind,
Then graveyard dust makes you clean.

So be like trees without branches,
Their roots decayed underground.

People are like water which is ruffled
And made one by the east wind.

Good men's actions are natural
While a scoundrel's charity
Is carefully planned to please.

A youth's long silence may seem
To be a sign of wisdom,
But it's really backwardness.

Though life is an unpaid loan,
We hope God will reward us.

I directed my concerns
To God; I failed to ask
If an eclipse might fall.
Many ignorant men
Save themselves from this death,
While thinkers hasten to it.

When an Indian burns himself,
He cremates his flesh and bones.
Does he fear holy torment,
Or the pressure of the grave
Upon his flat skeleton?

I was forced to come to this house of disaster,
But now I've settled here, I don't want to move.
I suffer terrible hardships; and there's no light
In men's temper. Clouds of rain, clouds of death,
Pass over populations which grow like plants.
Man lives by struggle; his mind is redundant.

The oddest event in life:
(God is neither forgetful,
Nor does he break his promises),
Two in bed become three.

The miser was hit by the cold.
He bitched about the hard weather,
And threw dinar after dinar
On his body hoping his wealth
Might warm him. Light your stored brazier,
Gold is not fire.

You said we've a wise creator
And I replied you're right, but look,
You claim he's timeless and nowhere.
Such terms, for all we know, could be
A secret language: which amounts
To saying we cannot think straight.

Needles have stitched a death shroud with our life
    thread;
It caps our temples. The searching intellect

Sees light as newly created and darkness
As the dimension from which it was born.

Don't pray for a kingdom in case you try
To seize power with force. Kings are sad creatures.

Each sunset warns quiet men who look ahead
That light will end; and each day postman Death

Knocks on our door. Although he does not speak,
He hands us a standing invitation.

Be like those skeleton horses which scent battle
And fear to eat. They wait chewing their bridles.

I'm surprised he's dead, and lies at rest.
He had many friends, and led a full life
With ups and downs, a weight in a balance.

If Aristotle's right, there's no room to house
The resurrected dead and all the unborn.

The world has groups: black and white, snow and tar.
Ham wasn't black because he sinned; God wished it.

Just as there are no people living in heaven,
No angels walk on earth, or lie buried.

Many nations have settled on other men's land,
Then fallen, and likewise crumbled into the soil.

Rack your memory for lost ancestors,
It can only tell you that they have gone.

If she believe or wear a cross,
Always be kind to your tired wife

Though she knocks religion and says:
'Friends, don't give a fig for old creeds,

People commit huge crimes having learnt
Only petty acts earn hell fire.'

Sin and crime, Raven, sin and crime,
They're all guilty; no creature's pure.

Take the food you need from the plains
And try to live in the treetops,

I'll not blame you. If your wings snuffed
Out the night light, I'd defend you.

Man frightens the lion in its den
And never gives the jackal any peace.

Thieves who tempt their neighbours to crime
Might as well hustle grapes to vineyards.

Man corrupts the life around him
And rats on friends who seek his help.

If you farmed man's estate, and made
It rich, stones would be your salary.

When I die I don't care how God
Treats the earth; let it parch, let it flood.

The earth doesn't know what it consumes:
Skeletons of sheep, carcases of lion.

The world is not to blame;
Therefore why blame the world?

Blame should fall on my head
And those like me. A glass

Holds wine; where does blame lie;
The man who presses the grape

Or he who drinks the wine?

Lord, when will I depart this world?
I've stayed too long. I don't know my star,
But since it circled, no friend expects
My help, no enemy my rage.
Life is youth's complaint; death cures it.
The earth is my bedroom, and yours;
No one has yet left his last home.

The soul driven from the body
Mourns the memory it leaves behind.

A dove hit in flight sadly turns
Its neck and sees its nest destroyed.

Chains of lightning turned the land of Beni
Silsilah★ from dust to acres of rich crops.

Towing cumulus clouds pregnant with rain
They drenched one land, and bypassed the next.

The storm washed my body of the dirt it held,
Yet it is my soul which needs to be cleansed.

My lips have never touched forbidden alcohol:
I don't harm my soul, my soul harms itself.

★ A tribe dwelling in Syria.

He does not light a fire behind my back,
I don't set the gorse ablaze when he leaves.

Journalists see planets in their darkness
As silver coins, and the sun a guinea.

I see mankind under two lights,
Past and future; and in two states,
Time and place. If we want to know
How God accounts for this oddness
We'll get an evasive answer.

The columns of life, the four elements,
Are pillars holding up the dome of stars.

God's two facts are fixed place and moving time.
Time has no concept of living creatures,

So why should it be blamed for what occurs?
Man is never tired of beautiful girls,

He waits his chance. Action wears out his body,
Yet action he needs to avoid boredom.

While fate threatens us we laugh and cry; but Time
Doesn't make us laugh or cry. Time which we curse

Has never intervened. If it could, it might
Have a word to say on how we behave.

We let the evil in us have its fling
And the most perverse is the most honest.

Day and night, two young men, go where we go:
No matter how we feel, they hang around.

His silver hair appeared like day,
But not like the dawn, or stars at night.

He speaks the words she doesn't want to hear,
The old man is nothing but phrases.

She wishes she could say to him,
'Take the dowry and be content';

Then she prays God will let him die,
But what young man will have her now?

Man is like fire which from a spark
Becomes a flame. Men on the land,

Men in towns are mutual servants,
Although the link may elude them.

Each part has its role: Hands can't walk,
Feet carry us. Hundreds of views

Exist about the world, and God
Who is ancient is the latest.

Store those good deeds which bring you joy
Or your days may end in sadness.